Nittany Lion's Journey Through The Keystone State

Aimee Aryal

Illustrated by Brent McCarthy

www.mascotbooks.com

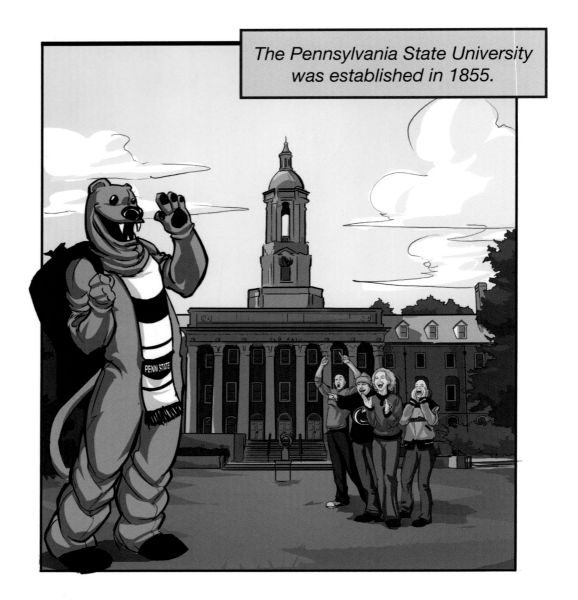

The Pennsylvania State University was established in 1855.

Nittany Lion was enjoying a relaxing summer on the campus of Penn State University. With football season fast approaching, Nittany Lion decided to take one last summer vacation. He thought it would be great fun to journey through the Keystone State and see many interesting places while making new friends along the way.

Before leaving campus, Nittany Lion strolled past Old Main. Penn State fans waved to him and yelled, "Hello, Nittany Lion!"

On his way out of town, Nittany Lion stopped at Beaver Stadium where he ran into Penn State fans. Everybody wished the mascot safe travels and said, "Enjoy your trip, Nittany Lion!"

Nittany Lion hopped into his blue and white car and hit the road!

From State College, Nittany Lion traveled east to the nearby Appalachian Trail. The mascot enjoyed spending time in the great outdoors so he went on a hike. As he enjoyed the natural beauty the region offered, Nittany Lion came across a bear. The bear growled, "Hello, Nittany Lion!"

At a lake, the mascot decided to go fishing. Nittany Lion hooked a big one! The fish gurgled in a worried voice, "Hello, Nittany Lion!"

From the Appalachian Trail, Nittany Lion continued east, stopping next at Hersheypark. The mascot loved riding roller coasters with fellow Penn State fans.

Nittany Lion posed for lots of pictures with his friends. "We are Penn State!" cheered the mascot's fans.

Hersheypark has eleven roller coasters.

At the arcade, the mascot played games with youngsters and had a great time. "You got the high score, Nittany Lion!" said a young fan.

Philadelphia was the mascot's next stop. There was so much to do and see in Philly! Nittany Lion's first stop was his favorite Philly Cheesesteak restaurant. Yummy!

Philadelphia is nicknamed the "City of Brotherly Love."

After filling up his stomach, Nittany Lion was ready to learn about American history. His first stop was Independence Hall. Then, it was onto the Liberty Bell. Everywhere the mascot went, he was greeted by Penn State fans. "Hello, Nittany Lion!" they cheered.

Nittany Lion was ready to experience more of the "City of Brotherly Love." He took in a Phillies baseball game and cheered the home team to victory.

Philadelphia is the sixth largest metropolitan area in America with nearly six million residents.

At the Philadelphia Museum of Art, Nittany Lion posed by the Rocky statue and raced up the stairs leading to the museum's entrance. Once inside, the mascot enjoyed all the fine artwork on display. His favorite piece was a portrait of George Washington. Seeing the portrait gave the mascot an idea for his own art project!

After loads of fun in Philadelphia, the mascot headed to Lancaster County. He was happy to make so many friends in Lancaster. While there, he helped a farmer plow his field. Tired horses neighed, "Hello, Nittany Lion!"

Lancaster County is nicknamed the "Garden Spot of America."

After waving goodbye to his new friends, Nittany Lion hopped back in his car and continued his journey through the Keystone State.

The Gettysburg Battlefield was the site of one of the most important battles of the Civil War.

Nittany Lion's next stop was Gettysburg. The mascot joined a Civil War reenactment at the Gettysburg National Military Park. His fellow soldiers were excited to see the mascot. They cheered, "Hello, Nittany Lion!"

The mascot toured this historic site with great interest. He especially enjoyed learning more about his favorite president, Abraham Lincoln.

From Gettysburg, the mascot made the long drive to Pittsburgh. His first stop in the "Steel City" was the Carnegie Museum of Natural History. Outside the museum, the mascot posed for pictures with young fans. Inside, Nittany Lion came face to face with a fierce Tyrannosaurus Rex. Yikes!

Pittsburgh was nicknamed the "Steel City" because of the city's steel industry.

The Pittsburgh Steelers have won a record six Super Bowl titles.

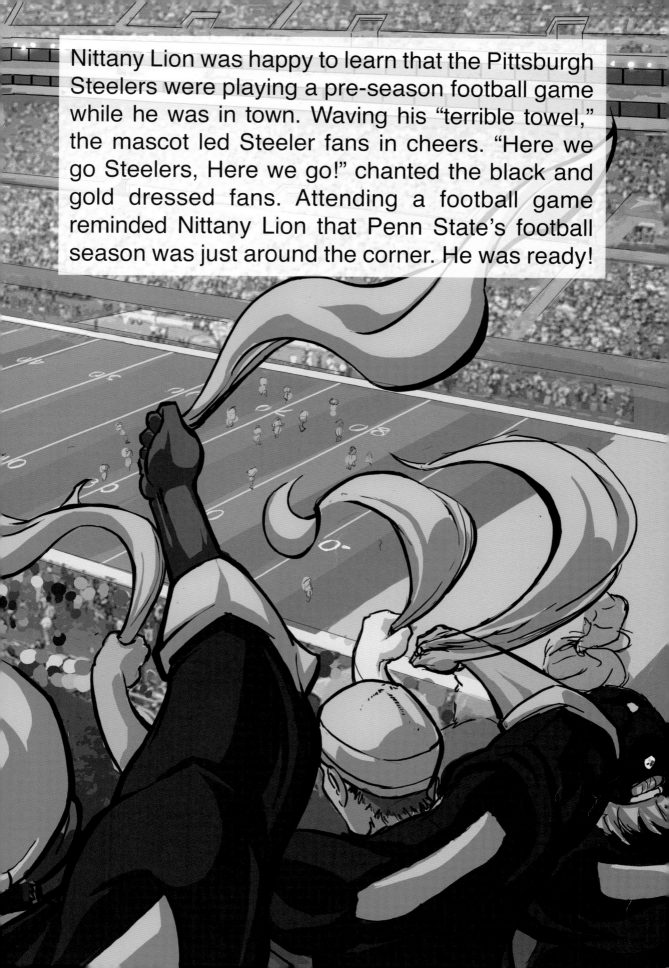

Nittany Lion was happy to learn that the Pittsburgh Steelers were playing a pre-season football game while he was in town. Waving his "terrible towel," the mascot led Steeler fans in cheers. "Here we go Steelers, Here we go!" chanted the black and gold dressed fans. Attending a football game reminded Nittany Lion that Penn State's football season was just around the corner. He was ready!

Erie is the fourth largest city in Pennsylvania and is on the shores of Lake Erie, one of the Great Lakes.

From Pittsburgh, Nittany Lion headed to the shores of Lake Erie. On the beach, the mascot helped a young Penn State fan build an amazing sand castle.

Next, Nittany Lion scaled a lighthouse and enjoyed spectacular views of the lake. He spotted a ship sailing in the distance and waved to the crew. He then boarded the Brig Niagara, which was docked in Erie, and imagined himself sailing around the world! Penn State fans spotted the mascot and cheered, "We are Penn State!"

Having traveled all over the Keystone State, Nittany Lion finally made it back to State College and the beautiful campus of Penn State. What a great trip it had been! His fans were thrilled at his return and cheered, "Hello, Nittany Lion! Welcome home!"

Back in his own room, Nittany Lion thought about all the interesting places he visited and the great friends he made along the way. He crawled into his own bed and fell fast asleep.

Good night, Nittany Lion!

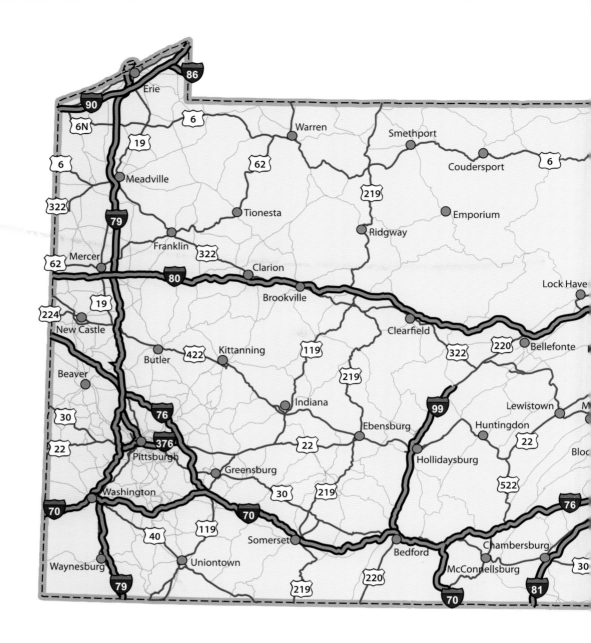

Nittany Lion's
Journey Through
The Keystone State

For Anna and Maya. ~ Aimee Aryal

To Dug-e-Fresh, Donnie B-B, Slick, my Babycakes,
and everyone in the NYC area who've been there to
support me during my stead. ~ Brent McCarthy

For more information about our products, please visit us online at www.mascotbooks.com.

For more information, please contact Mascot Books,
P.O. Box 220157, Chantilly, VA 20153-0157

ISBN: 1-934878-66-9

PRT0909A

Printed in the United States.

www.mascotbooks.com

Team	Title	Author
Boston Red Sox	Hello, *Wally*!	Jerry Remy
Boston Red Sox	*Wally The Green Monster* And His Journey Through *Red Sox Nation*!	Jerry Remy
Boston Red Sox	Coast to Coast with *Wally The Green Monster*	Jerry Remy
Boston Red Sox	A Season with *Wally The Green Monster*	Jerry Remy
Boston Red Sox	*Wally' The Green Monster And His* World Tour	Jerry Remy
Chicago Cubs	Let's Go, *Cubs*!	Aimee Aryal
Chicago White Sox	Let's Go, *White Sox*!	Aimee Aryal
Colorado Rockies	Hello, *Dinger*!	Aimee Aryal
Detroit Tigers	Hello, *Paws*!	Aimee Aryal
LA Angels	Let's Go, *Angels*!	Aimee Aryal
LA Dodgers	Let's Go, *Dodgers*!	Aimee Aryal
Milwaukee Brewers	Hello, *Bernie Brewer*!	Aimee Aryal
New York Yankees	Let's Go, *Yankees*!	Yogi Berra
New York Yankees	*Yankees* Town	Aimee Aryal
New York Mets	Hello, *Mr. Met*!	Rusty Staub
New York Mets	*Mr. Met* and his Journey Through the Big Apple	Aimee Aryal
Oakland Athletics	Let's Go, *A's*!	Aimee Aryal
Philadelphia Phillies	Hello, *Phillie Phanatic*!	Aimee Aryal
Cleveland Indians	Hello, *Slider*!	Bob Feller
San Francisco Giants	Go, *Giants*, Go!	Aimee Aryal
Seattle Mariners	Hello, *Mariner Moose*!	Aimee Aryal
St. Louis Cardinals	Hello, *Fredbird*!	Ozzie Smith
Washington Nationals	Hello, *Screech*!	Aimee Aryal

Team	Title	Author
Carolina Panthers	Let's Go, Panthers!	Aimee Aryal
Chicago Bears	Let's Go, Bears!	Aimee Aryal
Dallas Cowboys	How 'Bout Them Cowboys!	Aimee Aryal
Green Bay Packers	Go, Pack, Go!	Aimee Aryal
Kansas City Chiefs	Let's Go, Chiefs!	Aimee Aryal
Minnesota Vikings	Let's Go, Vikings!	Aimee Aryal
New York Giants	Let's Go, Giants!	Aimee Aryal
New York Jets	J-E-T-S! Jets, Jets, Jets!	Aimee Aryal
New England Patriots	Let's Go, Patriots!	Aimee Aryal
Pittsburg Steelers	Here We Go, Steelers!	Aimee Aryal
Seattle Seahawks	Let's Go, Seahawks!	Aimee Aryal

Basketball

Team	Title	Author
Dallas Mavericks	Let's Go, Mavs!	Mark Cuban
Boston Celtics	Let's Go, Celtics!	Aimee Aryal

Other

	Title	Author
National	Bo America's Commander In Leash	Naren Aryal
Kentucky Derby	White Diamond Runs For The Roses	Aimee Aryal
Marine Corps Marathon	Run, Miles, Run!	Aimee Aryal

College

School	Title	Author
Akron	Hello, Zippy	Jeremy Butler
Alabama	Hello, Big Al!	Aimee Aryal
Alabama	Roll Tide!	Ken Stabler
Alabama	Big Al's Journey Through the Yellowhammer State	Aimee Aryal
Arizona	Hello, Wilbur!	Lute Olson
Arizona State	Hello, Sparky!	Aimee Aryal
Arkansas	Hello, Big Red!	Aimee Aryal
Arkansas	Big Red's Journey Through the Razorback State	Aimee Aryal
Auburn	Hello, Aubie!	Aimee Aryal
Auburn	War Eagle!	Pat Dye
Auburn	Aubie's Journey Through the Yellowhammer State	Aimee Aryal
Boston College	Hello, Baldwin!	Aimee Aryal
Brigham Young	Hello, Cosmo!	LaVell Edwards
Cal - Berkeley	Hello, Oski!	Aimee Aryal
Cincinnati	Hello, Bearcat!	Mick Cronin
Clemson	Hello, Tiger!	Aimee Aryal
Clemson	Tiger's Journey Through the Palmetto State	Aimee Aryal
Colorado	Hello, Ralphie!	Aimee Aryal
Connecticut	Hello, Jonathan!	Aimee Aryal
Duke	Hello, Blue Devil!	Aimee Aryal
Florida	Hello, Albert!	Aimee Aryal
Florida	Albert's Journey Through the Sunshine State	Aimee Aryal
Florida State	Let's Go, 'Noles!	Aimee Aryal
Georgia	Hello, Hairy Dawg!	Aimee Aryal
Georgia	How 'Bout Them Dawgs!	Vince Dooley
Georgia	Hairy Dawg's Journey Through the Peach State	Vince Dooley
Georgia Tech	Hello, Buzz!	Aimee Aryal
Gonzaga	Spike, The Gonzaga Bulldog	Mike Pringle
Illinois	Let's Go, Illini!	Aimee Aryal
Indiana	Let's Go, Hoosiers!	Aimee Aryal
Iowa	Hello, Herky!	Aimee Aryal
Iowa State	Hello, Cy!	Amy DeLashmutt
James Madison	Hello, Duke Dog!	Aimee Aryal
Kansas	Hello, Big Jay!	Aimee Aryal
Kansas State	Hello, Willie!	Dan Walter
Kansas State	Willie the Wildcat's Journey Through the Kansas	Dan Walter
Kentucky	Hello, Wildcat!	Aimee Aryal
LSU	Hello, Mike!	Aimee Aryal
LSU	Mike's Journey Through the Bayou State	Aimee Aryal
Maryland	Hello, Testudo!	Aimee Aryal
Michigan	Let's Go, Blue!	Aimee Aryal
Michigan State	Hello, Sparty!	Aimee Aryal
Michigan State	Sparty's Journey Through Michigan	Aimee Aryal
Middle Tennessee	Hello, Lightning!	Aimee Aryal
Minnesota	Hello, Goldy!	Aimee Aryal
Mississippi	Hello, Colonel Rebel!	Aimee Aryal
Mississippi State	Hello, Bully!	Aimee Aryal
Missouri	Hello, Truman!	Todd Donoho
Missouri	Hello, Truman! Show Me Missouri!	Todd Donoho
Nebraska	Hello, Herbie Husker!	Aimee Aryal
North Carolina	Hello, Rameses!	Aimee Aryal
North Carolina	Rameses' Journey Through the Tar Heel State	Aimee Aryal
North Carolina St.	Hello, Mr. Wuf!	Aimee Aryal
North Carolina St.	Mr. Wuf's Journey Through North Carolina	Aimee Aryal
Northern Arizona	Hello, Louie!	Jeanette Ba
Notre Dame	Let's Go, Irish!	Aimee Aryal
Ohio State	Hello, Brutus!	Aimee Aryal
Ohio State	Brutus' Journey	Aimee Aryal
Oakland	Hello, Grizz!	Dawn Aubry
Oklahoma	Let's Go, Sooners!	Aimee Aryal
Oklahoma State	Hello, Pistol Pete!	Aimee Aryal
Oregon	Go Ducks!	Aimee Aryal
Oregon State	Hello, Benny the Beaver!	Aimee Aryal
Penn State	Hello, Nittany Lion!	Aimee Aryal
Penn State	We Are Penn State!	Joe Paterno
Purdue	Hello, Purdue Pete!	Aimee Aryal
Rutgers	Hello, Scarlet Knight!	Aimee Aryal
South Carolina	Hello, Cocky!	Aimee Aryal
South Carolina	Cocky's Journey Through the Palmetto State	Aimee Aryal
So. California	Hello, Tommy Trojan!	Aimee Aryal
Syracuse	Hello, Otto!	Aimee Aryal
Tennessee	Hello, Smokey!	Aimee Aryal
Tennessee	Smokey's Journey Through the Volunteer State	Aimee Aryal
Texas	Hello, Hook 'Em!	Aimee Aryal
Texas	Hook 'Em's Journey Through the Lone Star State	Aimee Aryal
Texas A & M	Howdy, Reveille!	Aimee Aryal
Texas A & M	Reveille's Journey Through the Lone Star State	Aimee Aryal
Texas Tech	Hello, Masked Rider!	Aimee Aryal
UCLA	Hello, Joe Bruin!	Aimee Aryal
Virginia	Hello, CavMan!	Aimee Aryal
Virginia Tech	Hello, Hokie Bird!	Aimee Aryal
Virginia Tech	Yea, It's Hokie Game Day!	Frank Bean
Virginia Tech	Hokie Bird's Journey Through Virginia	Aimee Aryal
Wake Forest	Hello, Demon Deacon!	Aimee Aryal
Washington	Hello, Harry the Husky!	Aimee Aryal
Washington State	Hello, Butch!	Aimee Aryal
West Virginia	Hello, Mountaineer!	Aimee Aryal
West Virginia	The Mountaineer's Journey Through West Virginia	Leslie H. Ha
Wisconsin	Hello, Bucky!	Aimee Aryal
Wisconsin	Bucky's Journey Through the Badger State	Aimee Aryal

SCHOOL PROGRAM

Promote reading. Build spirit. Raise money.™

Mascot Books® is creating customized children's books for public and private elementary schools all across America. Containing school-specific story lines and illustrations, our books are beloved by principals, librarians, teachers, parents, and of course, by young readers.

Our books feature your mascot taking a tour of your school, while highlighting all the things and events that make your school community such a special place.

The Mascot Books Elementary School Program is an innovative way to promote reading and build spirit, while offering a fresh, new marketing or fundraising opportunity.

Starting Is As Easy As 1-2-3!

1 You tell us all about your school community. What makes your school unique? What are your well-known traditions? Why do parents and students love your school?

2 With the information you share with us, Mascot Books creates a one-of-a-kind hardcover children's book featuring your school and your mascot.

3 Your book is delivered!

Great new fundraising idea for public schools!

Innovative way to market your private school to potential new students!

MASCOT BOOKS

www.mascotbooks.com

AUTHORS

If you have a book idea—no matter the subject—we'd like to hear from you.

What we do for Mascot Books® Authors

- Review your manuscript
- Character design and concept creation
- Illustrations
- Cover design and book layout
- Book printing
- Sales strategies

Why become a Mascot Books® Author?

- You retain full ownership of your story
- You set your own book price
- Getting a traditional publisher to take interest in your project is nearly impossible, and if they do, they take full control of your book and offer you a small royalty of 7% – 9%

From Here to There and Back With A Quack!

by Faith Nielsen

Little Kay Learns the Golden Rule

by Amir Mostafavi and Roya Mattis

Matt the Bat , Kitt the Mitt , and Paul the Ball

by Jim Rooker